THIS DECK CHAIR'S TAKEN
Issue nº 9 — Summer 2017

PART 1

The book as sun block, perfume, and puzzle, then a wide-ranging literary ramble with LILY COLE.

PART 2

Our Book of the Season is TREASURE ISLAND by Robert Louis Stevenson, with littoral pubs, parliamentary buccaneers, and instructions for finding a valuable hoard.

A pattern illustrating the mechanics of the figure-of-eight knot, a trusty friend of both sailors and pirates.

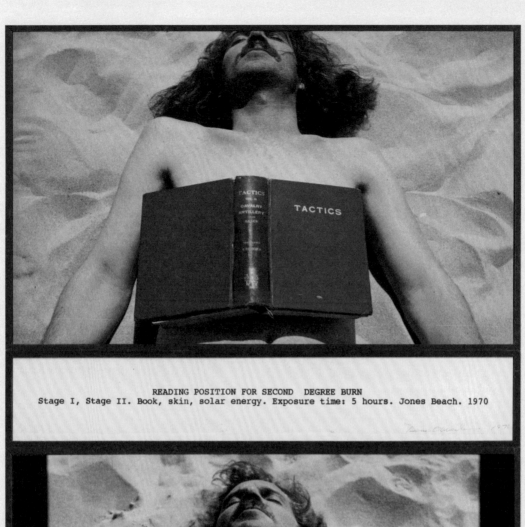

READING POSITION FOR SECOND DEGREE BURN
Stage I, Stage II. Book, skin, solar energy. Exposure time: 5 hours. Jones Beach. 1970

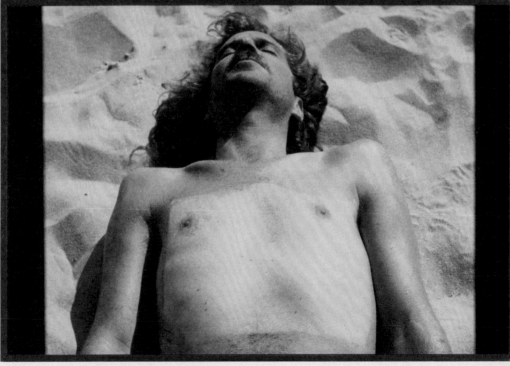

A large leather-bound book entitled *Tactics* blocks the sun in *Reading Position for Second Degree Burn*, an artwork by conceptual artist DENNIS OPPENHEIM.

SELF-IMPROVEMENT

'Keep going,' says the workout app. 'As you relax into 1 ment, you'll feel your hips open up.' The app tells us when to exercise, what to do. It exhorts us to carve out a little time, three, four, five times a week. We obey it for health reasons and the so-called 'rush of endorphins', but there's something else there — a restorative quality about these private blocks of time, filled as they are with nothing except basic, repetitive action. While the app orders us to plank-walk and rock our quads, we are away from worry, away from the Haribo-binge of breaking news, away from the passive-aggressive assault course of twenty-first-century mood maintenance. 'Keep going,' says the running app. 'Keep going,' says the mindfulness app. 'Keep going,' says the teach-yourself-a-language app.

There is no motivational app for reading. Unlike with exercise and 'self-improvement', we are meant to just... do it. To want to do it. How vulgar, to need a 'regime' for enjoying books. But still. Reading's enemy is the same as that of learning Swahili: not lack of intent but belief in a time-rich future that never arrives. Which is why some do treat it like running, in the sense of ruthlessly carving out the time no matter what. Art curator Hans Ulrich Obrist told us last summer that, to jump-start his ever-busy mind, he reads for fifteen minutes every day, without fail, the moment he wakes up. Others find a sense of literary purpose in the personal touch of offline book-buying and will mention 'my bookseller' the same way one might speak about 'my personal trainer'. What they mean is they made friends with someone at the bookshop who knows their tastes, recommends them material, and enquires how they found the last batch. Is this what's behind the resurgence of the bricks-and-mortar bookshop? Something is.

The comparison has its limits, of course. One workout changes us for a couple of days then fades; a single book might influence us for the rest of our lives. 'Keep going,' *The Happy Reader* would say, if its world weren't a thousand times more interesting than that.

Bookish Magazine
Issue n° 9 — Summer 2017

The Happy Reader is
a collaboration between
Penguin Books and
Fantastic Man

EDITOR-IN-CHIEF
Seb Emina

EDITORIAL DIRECTORS
Jop van Bennekom
Gert Jonkers

MANAGING EDITOR
Maria Bedford

DESIGN
Tom Etherington
Matthew Young

DESIGN CONCEPT
Jop van Bennekom
Helios Capdevila

PICTURE RESEARCH
Samantha Johnson

PRODUCTION
Imogen Scott

PUBLISHER
Helen Conford

MARKETING DIRECTOR
Nicola Hill

BRAND DIRECTOR
Sam Voulters

MANAGING DIRECTOR
Stefan McGrath

CONTRIBUTORS
Jeremy Allen, Jean Hannah
Edelstein, Eliot Haworth, Ishion
Hutchinson, Jordan Kelly, Penny
Martin, Yelena Moskovich,
Dennis Oppenheim, Daniel
Rachel, Nicholas Rankin, Rosa
Rankin-Gee, Ivan Ruberto,
Megan Wray Schertler, David
Benjamin Sherry, Amelia Tait,
Wolfgang Tillmans.

THANK YOU
Magnus Åkesson, Isabelle De Cat,
Travis Elborough, Sophie Harris,
Paula Karaiskos, Rebecca Lee,
Rebecca Morris, Caroline Pretty.

Penguin Books
80 Strand
London WC2R 0RL

info@thehappyreader.com
www.thehappyreader.com

SNIPPETS

Sun-blushed susurrations on books, readers and related happenings.

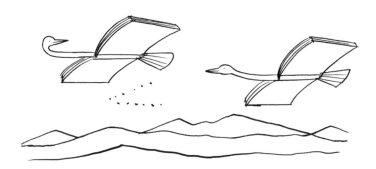

STORAGE — Norway has taken the precautionary step of establishing a 'doomsday library'. Located around 800 miles from the North Pole on the island of Spitsbergen, not far from a similar structure for the preservation of seeds, the World Arctic Archive uses film technology that can preserve a book for up to 1,000 years. Wedged deep into permafrost, the library should theoretically remain open to visitors even after a nuclear war.

*

CRIME — A man walked into a bookshop and destroyed several books by Kim Kardashian. Carl Puia, aged seventy-four, poured 'red liquid' over six copies of *Selfish*, Kardashian's coffee-table collection of selfies, before presenting himself to the local police station in Glastonbury, Connecticut.

*

COUNTRY PILE — The musician and author Patti Smith has purchased a reconstruction of Arthur Rimbaud's childhood home. The house is in the village of Roche, in the Ardennes region of France, where during the mid 1870s, aged just nineteen, the poet wrote his best-known work, *A Season in Hell*. Smith has spoken of Rimbaud as a lifelong influence.

*

WOW — An English professor in Ontario was irritated to misplace her copy of a favourite academic book entitled *Consuming Subjects*. Years later, she ordered a replacement copy online and when it arrived, she found her own name handwritten on the title page — it was her missing copy.

ESQUE — An interesting video game based on the writings of Franz Kafka, author of *The Trial* and *Metamorphosis*, has been released. *The Franz Kafka Videogame* is by Dennis Galanin, a lone game developer working out of Yekaterinburg, the administrative centre of Sverdlovsk Oblast, Russia. It is available for PC and iPhone.

*

TYPE CAST — American actor Tom Hanks is to publish his first book, a collection of short stories themed around typewriters.

*

PERFUME — Timothy Han, a former assistant to John Galliano who reinvented himself as a much-feted perfumer, is concocting a line of scents inspired by classic novels. She Came to Stay, based on the 1943 Simone de Beauvoir novel, became a runaway olfactory bestseller, and he described his follow-up, On the Road, from the Jack Kerouac novel, as being 'like the road trip, starting in New York and going all the way through America.' Now he is launching a scent based on Yukio Mishima's *The Decay of the Angel* (1971).

*

MAXIMUM RARE — London-based rare book dealer Pom Harrington of Peter Harrington Rare Books was surprised to be offered a 'first edition' of *The Iliad*. The epic poem by Homer dates back to sometime between 760 and 710 BC, around 2,000 years before the invention of the printing press in 1440. 'It's not something you're likely to stumble across outside an archaeological site,' said Harrington.

*

TIME MACHINE — The Barbican Centre in London is to hold a 'festival-style exhibition' dedicated to science-fiction. Amid alien galleries and spacesuit displays will be a plethora of books, manuscripts and typescripts from authors including Octavia Butler, who, in 1998, devised a character named Senator Andrew Steele, 'a demagogue', who in the year 2032 rallies his crowds with the call to 'Make America Great Again!' *Into the Unknown* runs from 3 June until 1 September.

*

HABITS — Justin Trudeau, Prime Minister of Canada, revealed some of his favourite authors to users of the 'knowledge-sharing' website Quora. The literature graduate and former snowboard instructor is a fan of horror guru Stephen King, sword-and-sorcery purveyor Tad Williams and cyberpunk maestro Neal Stephenson.

*

MATCH — Film director Barry Jenkins, winner of this year's Best Picture Oscar for *Moonlight*, is to work on a movie adaptation of Colson Whitehead's *The Underground Railroad*, winner of this year's Pulitzer Prize for Fiction.

How the devil does she do it? Screen-acting, super-modelling, stage-performing, bookshop-owning, technology start-up founding, philanthropic project-creating and who knows what else: just reading about it is exhausting. For others any of these would constitute an entire career, a life's work, but for 29-year-old LILY COLE they are simply expressions of globe-striding ambition combined with a mighty intellect.

As she gazes from her apartment window in London, Cole sees a world where the best is yet to come. As per this *Happy Reader* interview, taking place over two extended sessions in her home city, incredibly she still finds time to delve into books — everything from classic literature to popular science — for ideas and inspiration that might set off yet more projects, yet more parallel careers.

LILY COLE

In conversation with
PENNY MARTIN

Portraits by
WOLFGANG TILLMANS

LILY LUAHANA COLE
(27-12-87)

Born in Torquay, Devon. Sisters: 2. Discovered by Storm Models aged 14. Studied BA History of Art at Kings College, Cambridge (grade: double first). Acting roles include: *The Imaginarium of Doctor Parnassus* and *Absolutely Fabulous: The Movie*. Star sign: Capricorn. Daughters: 1. Height: 179cm. Shoe size: 6. Books written: 1. Bookshops owned: 1.

We photographed Cole at her home in London, and around St Pancras International and Kings Cross stations: nice and handy for both Paris and Peterborough.

LONDON

The first time I met Lily Cole she was in her school tracksuit, loitering in the corridors of a north-west London photo studio. The website I then edited was staging a shoot next door involving nudity, fetish costumes, and a live performance from Alexander McQueen. Concerned about what this fresh-faced fourteen-year-old might witness, a colleague and I approached her. Was she looking for her mum, we ventured? Actually, replied Cole with an unmistakable hint of self-possession, she was here to work. The future Model of the Year (2004) went on to steal the show in a (chaste) girl-turns-into-woman performance. She was booked for her first *Vogue* cover the following year.

For Cole, work and education have always coexisted harmoniously. While at the height of her powers as a model and actress, with a leading role in Terry Gilliam's *The Imaginarium of Doctor Parnassus*, she happily took three years out to get her degree at King's College, Cambridge. These days, as co-founder of the sharing-economy platform Impossible, co-owner of beloved London bookshop Claire de Rouen, and face of numerous philanthropic causes, from saving Asian elephants to ending child labour, Cole is able to make full use of her penchant for books in the array of fields in which she operates.

Our 2017 reunion, beginning at a nearby theatre-world haunt, the Ivy, occurs between rehearsals of her latest play, *The Philanthropist*. Now twenty-nine and in a belted camel coat and checked grandpa slippers with her signature flame-coloured hair gathered in a top knot, Cole exercises her credentials as PETA's Sexiest Vegetarian of 2013 by ordering lunch off-menu. She's been mostly vegan for the past year and is feeling all the better for it.

PENNY: I'm coming to see *The Philanthropist* tonight.

LILY: Oh, are you? I hope you like it. It's in previews. Do you know much about theatre — that you have a few weeks of previews before you open officially?

P: I didn't realise it was so many.

L: It depends. In America, they have like a month of them. But we've got two and a half weeks, which we're halfway through already.

P: How much can a play change during that time?

L: As much as is necessary. This one probably won't change a lot

1. READ THE PLAY
—
Sales of playscripts rocketed last year thanks largely to the opening of *Harry Potter and the Cursed Child* in London's West End. Publishing industry analysts Nielsen BookScan reported the wizarding stage play had become the biggest selling edition of any script since records began, with 847,886 copies sold in the first week alone. In distant second is Shakespeare's *Romeo and Juliet* with 127,726 copies sold since 1998.

2. SPANNERS INTO THE WORKS
—
This phrase, evoking the mayhem caused by lobbing a wrench into the gears of running machinery, is thought to have been coined by P. G. Wodehouse in his upper-class caper *Right Ho, Jeeves*, published in 1934.

because we'd already spent a month rehearsing it before we went into the theatre, Trafalgar Studios. Now, it's more like nuancing. We're in every day with the director.

P: Is that Simon Callow?

L: Yes. He's quite wonderful. I hadn't met him before and I had no preconceptions but he's somebody I would probably want to be friends with in a different context — very smart and interesting and generous of spirit. Also a complete trove of industry knowledge.

P: He certainly seems entertaining. I sat close to him in Sheekey's one night and he had his table in hysterics for the full three courses.

L: He's brilliant. And to have a director who is an actor first and foremost is quite unusual. There's quite a difference. I don't want to generalise, but a lot of directors I've worked with know when a performance is working or not working but they can't necessarily help you get there. So it's quite special to have somebody who is complicit in creating the performance with you. Simon's very detail-orientated, right down to the 'ums' and 'ers' and the intonation on lines. Have you read the play?

P: No. And I'm not sure if I've seen it either. I saw the Molière one it was written in response to, *The Misanthrope*, years ago.

L: OK, well, it's set on a university campus and the seven characters are all lecturers and students, several of whom are old friends. Then me and one other character, Braham, come from nowhere, throw spanners into the works, and all their stories unravel. The characters are based on the seven deadly sins. I think that's a little-known fact. My character, Araminta, is lust.

P: Well, I'm looking forward to seeing it all the more! Do you see a lot of theatre? I'm told more money is being spent on theatre tickets in London than on cinema tickets.

L: Really? That's exciting. I go in and out of phases. Right now, I like *Travesties*, Tom Stoppard's play at the Apollo. What else? I went to see four plays in the two weeks before we started on *The Philanthropist*, just to get into the spirit of things. I think the two I enjoyed most were *Who's Afraid of Virginia Woolf?* at the Harold Pinter Theatre. An old school friend of mine was playing the younger character...

P: Who's that?

L: Imogen Poots. We did our A levels together at Latymer Upper School in Hammersmith. Imelda Staunton was playing the lead and she gave an unbelievably amazing performance. It was a really good play. And then I went to see *Hedda Gabler* at the National and I thought that was brilliant. I'd say *Jerusalem* probably goes down as one of my favourite plays ever. I saw it three times, originally at the Royal Court, then in New York and then back here in London.

P: That all sounds very earnest, Lily. You're not a fan of musicals?

L: I saw *The Book of Mormon*, actually, which is really worth going to see.

P: We're here to discuss books, which we'll come to, but first of all I'm interested in all the other kinds of reading you're required to do as part of your job. Jobs, actually, as you seem to have so many. How do scripts find their way to you?

L: I don't know. Mostly through my agent, Lindy King.

P: She reads them for you before you see them?

L: Yes. But often she doesn't even need to because she knows whether it's interesting based on the director, the people who are attached to the project, the producers.

P: So the play is judged according to a sort of strategic set of criteria before you're responding to the text?

L: Kind of. They wouldn't just send me anything. Then I often send scripts to my sister. Unfortunately, there's not that much great material. That's part of the struggle. And then when there is strong material, everyone else is on it. I'm increasingly interested in either trying to write stuff myself, or commission stuff that I'm interested in, acting more as a producer. I know a lot of actors who are doing that.

P: Explain to me how the conversation went between you and your agent when she gave you the script for *The Philanthropist*.

L: I'd heard of Christopher Hampton and I'd heard of Simon Callow, but I'd never read the play. I guess one of the things that attracted me to it is that it's taking the piss out of the bourgeois, often quite self-righteous thinking that can accompany philanthropy.

P: There's a neat link between the play's title and all the philanthropic work for which you are known.

L: Ha, a journalist actually asked me the other day whether that's why I'd taken the part! There's a big space between reading a play and seeing one performed. I got that this one was really well written, but I didn't quite get the comedy from what was on the page. You realise it's full of jokes once you see it performed. But they're embedded deep in the text, which is what so impresses me about Christopher

3. SIMON CALLOW
—
Simon Callow's acting credits from 1987, the year of Cole's birth, include High Renaissance engraver Marcantonio Raimondi in a TV screenplay about painter Giovanni Cariani, murdered museum director Theodore Kemp in the *Inspector Morse* episode 'The Wolvercote Tongue' and the voice of a dragon in children's animation *The Reluctant Dragon*.

Hampton. You think, 'How could you trust people were going to get it?' He says it was the hardest thing he ever wrote.

P: Why?

L: He just found comedy really hard to write. I mean, his most famous three works are the screenplays for *Dangerous Liaisons*, *A Dangerous Method* and *Atonement*. I actually watched *Dangerous Liaisons* last night. It's so brilliantly awful. I'm not even a fan of period things normally.

P: Do the 1980s count as 'period'? I saw you're in the new film of Martin Amis's book *London Fields*. When is that coming out?

L: Oh, haven't you heard? We finished filming years ago but the director, Mathew Cullen, fell out with the Hanleys, the producers, and now we're not sure it will ever come out.

P: That's a shame! I was looking forward to seeing you play Trish Shirt. Isn't she the dreaded Keith Talent's sex slave?

L: Yeah! It's a small part but it was really fun. They made me look completely awful in it — I think that's the worst I've ever looked!

P: You've done quite a number of cameos — I counted seventeen performances as 'Self' on IMDb, from films like *The September Issue* to appearances on news programmes.

L: I played myself in *Absolutely Fabulous: The Movie* just after having my daughter in 2015, which was a really nice way to come back to work. I'd grown up watching it on TV, so I had a lot of affection for it. I've actually got a really small part in the next Star Wars movie...

P: You're kidding — *The Last Jedi*? Is that a lifelong dream fulfilled?

L: Maybe Harry Potter was more meaningful to me. I'd fallen in love with those books long before the films were made. But I went back and watched every one of the Star Wars films when I got the part and I was really into them by the time I arrived on set. It's just a tiny role. I'm barely in it.

P: Even so, I'm star-struck! I read you started acting very young. Aged six.

L: I went to theatre school, Sylvia Young, for a while. My family had noticed how much I enjoyed performing. But I wouldn't say I learned anything of particular... quality there. I transferred back to a regular primary school pretty quickly. Still, it was an early indication of how much I enjoyed it, and I continued acting throughout school. Then when I was sixteen, once I was modelling, Marilyn Manson asked me to play Alice in a production of *Alice's Adventures in Wonderland* that he was directing. You can see it online.

P: How did you learn technical things like memorising your lines? Do you favour the sing-song method?

L: Touch wood, as I'm on stage tonight, I've been pretty good at all that. I couldn't recite you poetry or anything, but my short-term memory is pretty good.

P: Once a play gets into its run, there's quite a bit of down time in the day — sometimes between scenes, even. Have you a book on the go to keep you occupied?

L: Since we're still rehearsing there's not really been a spare moment. But recently I've been getting into audiobooks, and I can listen to those when I'm doing my make-up and so on. I prefer a printed book, but I'll read from whatever's available: tablet, whatever.

P: I tried audiobooks — the artist Lucy McKenzie is fanatical about Audible.com and encouraged me to download *Middlemarch*, which I'd never read. But I noticed I was only really absorbing 60% of what I was hearing, which is no good if it's something really detailed like George Eliot. I was always having to pause my run to skip back to clarify plot points and identify mystery characters.

L: I think it depends on whether you're allocating specific time for them, when you're not engaged in anything else that's too diverting. I recently audio-read Yuval Harari's *Sapiens* during a long car ride.

P: Wow, you covered the entire history of the human race in a single car journey?

L: Yes, it was great! Really detailed, but I think I got most of it. I'm now on to his new one, *Homo Deus*, though I notice I'm not quite so gripped once I'm out of the car.

P: Perhaps it's also something to do with who narrates the audiobook. Are you more of a Stephen Fry or a Juliet Stevenson kind of listener?

L: I don't think I'm looking for specific personalities, but I do listen to the thirty-second clip before I buy the book, in case I can't stand the person's voice. It would be quite good fun to narrate one, I think. When I think of it, I've started quite a few audiobooks recently...

P: So you're a promiscuous reader? I'm more of a serial monogamist when it comes to books.

L: Polyamorous, maybe. If I've a few going concurrently, it probably means that no one of them has gripped me in particular. In the

4. SAPIENS

—

Surprisingly successful in its ambition to recount the complete history of humankind in a single highly readable tome, Harari's book is one of the great non-fiction phenomena of our time. His argument that our species has dominated the planet thanks to its ability to dream up fictional entities — from myths to legal systems to nation states — is a notion that speaks fascinatingly to the potency of books.

last year, though, the company that I'm part of, Impossible, has been working with Google on producing a book that's built on the block-chain. And that has been fascinating. It's called *A Universe Explodes*.

P: Hang on, I think a friend sent me a link to that this week. Is this the one written by Tea Uglow at Google's Creative Labs? To be honest, I couldn't quite make out what to do with it.

L: Yes, I saw Tea yesterday and she gave me one of the first hundred copies. Here, let me show it to you on my phone. So... this is the first page. As one of the owners of the book, I can delete two words of every page and add one word.

P: So every owner is a contributor to the final edit? Fun! Does that mean we're co-authors?

L: Yes! There are twenty-one pages and we go through every one, adding a word, deleting two. Then you give the book to someone else and they do the same thing. Because you're deleting one word more than you're adding, it means it's gradually getting smaller and smaller and smaller until there is just one word left on each page.

P: And what final form will that take? Is this purely a virtual exercise?

L: I don't think they're going to print it. Tea's fascinating. I think her question is one of ownership: whether you can ever own a literary work. She would argue that with a digital book, you're never owning it; you're only ever licensing it.

P: I enjoyed looking at the list of your favourite books.

L: Oh, you got that? Sorry it came in texts and email fragments — I kept thinking of more. There's so much to discuss when it comes to reading, it turns out.

P: *Ada or Ardor* is a title you've often cited in interviews as your all-time favourite. When I was at university in the early '90s, it was a set text, along with *Lolita*. Some students were completely scandalised by the incestuous subject matter — one woman refused to finish it.

L: For me, the genius of Nabokov is down to his use of language. Every paragraph is rich with different meanings and symbolism.

P: Isn't there some sort of colour symbolism in the title — the A was the yellow and the D the black of his favourite butterfly or something?

L: I thought it was the shape of the word. Aren't the As like wings on either side of the D body? And then you fall in love with the characters; there's something very seductive about this impossible relationship. For me, what's so powerful with both *Lolita* and *Ada* is

5. BLOCKCHAIN
—
The original utility of the so-called blockchain, which widely distributes a publicly-checkable digital database, was to create online verifiability and trust for the cryptocurrency Bitcoin. Earlier this year the price of one Bitcoin hit an all-time high of $1277.65.

how he draws you into a scenario that's definitely transgressive by normal moral standards — paedophilia and incest — but he makes it so human that he brings you into their world and their perspective. I mean, you definitely wouldn't want Ada and Van to be together.

P: Am I right in remembering that at the beginning of the book they don't know they are siblings?

L: Yes, and what's so brilliant is that as a reader, you don't know either. There are murmurs of it early on, but you're not sure. I think that's interesting because I really love empathy and non-judgement as practices. I think one of the things that draws me towards acting is the challenge to try and see myself in people whom I might ordinarily judge and condemn from the outset. Nabokov definitely expands your mind in that respect. Which of the books I listed was the one you said we had a difference of opinion over? Was it *The Argonauts*?

P: Yes! How did you guess?

L: That's the only one that's vaguely polarising.

P: Really? I've not yet met anyone that didn't like it. And I should add that I didn't not like it. I just think I chose the wrong time to read it. I raced through it by the pool in Greece — completely the wrong context for something that felt like a bit of a lesson.

L: Being lectured to, mmm. I felt like it was a lesson, yes, but that's kind of what I loved about it.

P: I noticed there's a didactic quality to some of the books you listed.

L: I like things that either make my imagination fly, that transport me to a different world, or things that I learn a new perspective from. It's very rare to read something that shifts your opinion on an issue. And I thought *The Argonauts* was beautifully written. Maggie Nelson's use of language really drew me in. It also has an unusual structure — memoir mixed with non-fiction.

P: Have you read Ariel Levy's new book, *The Rules Do Not Apply*?

L: No.

P: Again, it's a very personal memoir from a feminist author who quite possibly never thought they were going to write a memoir. I don't know if you saw her earlier *New Yorker* piece about her miscarriage when reporting in Mongolia...

L: Oh God, no.

P: ...and her reflections on the limits of what's actually possible, even

6. THE ARGONAUTS
—

The title of Maggie Nelson's book *The Argonauts* (2015) is about love, in reference to the French literary theorist Roland Barthes' assertion that when we say 'I love you' we are like 'the Argonaut renewing his ship during its voyage without changing its name.' Said Nelson: 'Just as the *Argo*'s parts may be replaced over time but the boat is still called the *Argo*, whenever the lover utters the phrase "I love you," its meaning must be renewed by each use.'

Cole has been called a Renaissance woman, both for the polymathic tendencies she holds and her undeniably oil painting-like qualities, visible even as she relaxes on a comfortable fake mushroom.

for the most emancipated of working women who want a family. That same text forms a crucial part of the book.

L: Interesting. I must look it up.

P: I saw it was taken apart by Charlotte Shane in the *New Republic* for being 'entitled', which I thought was unwarranted. It really bothers me when that word is used to silence people, though I possibly use it a bit myself.

L: The danger of criticising literature from a moral perspective is that inevitably you're opening yourself up to criticisms of hypocrisy. Obviously, in the UK most people are privileged in comparison with the world at large. There's a line in *The Philanthropist* from Braham's character, which is played by Matt Berry. The background joke is that he left the left wing 'for tax reasons'. So he's a bit of an arsehole, but in some ways it's charming because he's honest with himself about it. He says, 'You have two choices. You can either keep it, or give it all away.' i.e. there's no middle ground. I am definitely interested in critiquing the bubbles we all live in.

P: That was the message behind Impossible, when you launched it in 2011. At that stage, I'd understood it as a sort of barter economy operated via your website.

L: Now it's a bit more like Tinder for sharing. In the last year we've rebuilt the platform so now it's an app, via which you can post things and services that you can give, and things that you want help with. The idea is that we match those offers and requests based on friends, locations, skills, et cetera.

P: Is that what makes it different from a craigslist — the fact that you act as the conduit?

L: Exactly. What we've done recently is work with a really good engineering firm, Pivotal Labs, to open-source it so anybody can take that code and develop it.

P: I used to edit a website, and all that development time sounds very expensive to me.

L: Oh God, yes, and a lot of work.

P: Is Impossible a money drain?

L: It has been in the past.

P: Have you spent all your money on it?

L: I put in as much as I could, yes, and we also had some money from the government via a grant, and then we also had pro bono work. Had I been charging for my time... I dread to think. Until last year I was pretty much full-time. But when I took time off to have my daughter, I took stock and I was like, I really don't enjoy being on my computer all the time, dealing with emails and all the logistical aspects of running a business. That wasn't why I'd gotten into it at all.

P: People have no idea about all the hidden work involved in running a website.

L: So my partner...

P: Is that Kwame Ferreira?

L: Yeah, he and I restructured our companies in such a way that Impossible can essentially run without me. And in the process, we've produced good tech that's available for the next crazy person who likes the idea to take and fly with. I mean, Impossible hasn't had the world-shattering effect that I hoped it might in the beginning, but it may in future, in quieter ways. Using the tech to empower communities in universities, for example, or different community groups. When we started six years ago, you hadn't even heard of the 'sharing economy'. I remember when I was looking at our predecessors, like Airbnb, for example — no one had heard of it. That was a really well-designed version of the concept and obviously, that's now exploded. I think we're at the beginning of a phase of seeing how technology can change trade relationships in a positive way.

P: I noticed you're working on products and brand development as well as the sharing activities.

L: Yes, now it's more like an ecosystem. The sharing app still loses money, but now that can be subsidised by other parts of the business. The products and so on are more my partner's side of things.

P: What sorts of things do you sell?

L: Things from The North Circular for one, the company I set up in 2009 with my friend Katherine Poulton, the knitwear designer.

P: I loved that project!

L: Yes, Katherine's lovely. But we were totally naive. I think if either of us had known what we both know now, how difficult it is to run a business and make it successful, we probably wouldn't have done it. At that time, I was working a lot on ethical fashion, and was enthusiastic about the idea of trying to make consumers think about the impact of the products that we touch and use every day and the stories behind them. In a non-preachy way, you know, just like, 'This jumper was knitted by this person.' Originally, we were going to say,

7. THE NORTH CIRCULAR
—
A fashion company founded after Cole and Poulton had an idea to utilise the unparalleled hand-knitting skills of grandmothers to knit clothing from the wool of rare breed Wensleydale sheep, known to be the most lustrous in the world.

'The wool comes from this sheep, and this is the shepherd, and this is the knitter...'

P: You were responsible for writing all the text on the website too? Are you a fast writer?

L: Yes, I think I'm quite a fast writer but quite a slow reader.

P: Is that because you're really poring over the words? You've mentioned language as a motivation for reading particular writers.

L: Yes, maybe.

P: I'm definitely slower when it's out of obligation. When I started as an editor, I went through a phase of feeling guilty about reading for pleasure. I always felt I should be going through a contributor's copy instead and so rarely touched anything 'non essential' like fiction, which of course was ridiculous.

L: I don't think I ever feel guilty about reading. If anything, I feel guilty about what I'm *not* reading. In that respect, one of the most interesting books I've started recently is by a friend, Dr James Suzman; it's called *Affluence Without Abundance*. He's an anthropologist who's worked a lot with the Bushmen in Botswana, studying 'primitive affluence' and what we can learn from these cultures. I'm only part of the way into it, but so far he's arguing that Bushmen actually lived a very wealthy existence — they worked shorter weeks than us, foraging and hunter-gathering. Much more time was devoted to leisure and enjoying life. He says the most sustainable futures will require us to change our cultural perspectives on whether we need objects at all, as opposed to focusing on designing perfect objects, ethically or not. I was given another book by a publisher friend, which isn't too dissimilar, called *Utopia for Realists*. I wrote my thesis at university about utopias.

P: Did you? Utopias as abstract concepts or real places?

L: Well, I looked at the etymology of 'utopia', which means 'a good place' and 'no place' in Greek. What interests me is that for so long we've largely understood 'utopia' as a construct that's impossible to achieve.

P: In the way that, say, Thomas More uses it?

L: Exactly. More was inverting it, almost using it as a pun — implying that the good place is no place at all. But if you flip that idea and say, no, the good place doesn't exist physically, then you're saying that there is such a thing as utopia, at least in the abstract. It's just the essence of possibility in the present moment.

8. UTOPIA

—

One way of creating a real utopia is to simply give a place the name Utopia, as per the tiny town Utopia (population: 227), Uvalde County, Texas. Utopia is home to a nice swimming hole with a rope swing.

P: Aha, which of course you're referencing or inverting in the title of your company, Impossible. I was looking at the magazine you're making. Is it called *Impossible to Print*?

L: Yes. We've only made one so far; it came out last year. I think we'll make it an annual affair. We were starting to stage a lot of talks and other activities at Impossible and were accumulating a lot of content that had no place to go.

P: It's quite provocative and zine-y, with its 'anger is an energy' centrefold montage. I read that the creative direction is based on *The Impossible Dream* fanzine produced at the start of the '80s by the famous Lance d'Boyle of Poison Girls. I ordered one from Impossible.com.

L: You should have said, I'd have brought one! Well, that's really the editor, Graham Erickson's input. We're on to the next one now.

P: Do you subscribe to any magazines?

L: No, I don't.

P: That's probably a consequence of modelling: photo studios are usually heaving with all the current issues — why would you buy one? Plus you must see them all at the bookshop you run, Claire de Rouen.

L: Well, our titles are more angled towards art photography.

P: Do you think that's where the printed form excels?

L: I don't think print is better or worse than digital; there are advantages to both. And I don't run the bookshop, FYI, I just turn up occasionally. But we do a book fair called Room&Book at the ICA once a year and that's amazing, to see all these rare, physical objects. With photo books, there's a degree of quality to the images that you would never achieve digitally. And then lots of the books are massive or have weird shapes. That physical specificity's less critical with literary books, although there's still something really special about holding one in your hands and being able to underline words on the page or whatever. Do you know who Clement Greenberg is?

P: The editor of *Partisan Review*?

L: I don't know that one, but in 1939 he wrote an article called 'Avant-Garde and Kitsch', talking about the impact of photography and how art was in danger of being relegated to kitsch — entertainment, basically. But Greenberg argued that what art could do in the face of the rise of this new photographic medium was to defend what was unique to art. To painting especially — its materiality. That in reality, Rothko and Jackson Pollock were making an object, as opposed to an object that's pretending to be a person or a tree.

9. POISON GIRLS
—
Anarcho-punk band Poison Girls first played together in 1975 for a semi-improvised show at the Edinburgh Fringe Festival that *The Scotsman* described as 'worse than two hours of toothache.' The Brighton-formed group went on to perform together for ten years, and their records remain sought-after treasures.

P: So you're a modernist bookseller, is that what you're saying?

L: Ha, not necessarily! I just think in the same way that art de-fended itself against the threat of photography by showing that it pro-vides a value beyond mere representation, books have an opportunity to benefit from the challenges of digital through presenting them-selves as meaningful objects that offer something different to what you're going to get from a Kindle or iPad.

P: I see you recently judged a competition for Kindle.

L: Yes, I was on the award panel for the Amazon Kindle Story-teller project this year. The winners will be announced in July.

P: Who can enter that?

L: Anybody, which is what I really like about it. You don't have to be previously published, which is the case with a lot of the other big book awards. All you have to do is self-publish a book of over 5,000 words through their platform, Kindle Direct Publishing. The winner gets £20,000 and, I guess, lots of marketing for their story. Appar-ently, more books are now self-published than via major publishing houses. My mum's a writer...

P: Is she? What's her name?

L: Patience Owen. She writes fiction and poetry, and she's very, very good. I've been encouraging her to self-publish, as I think in the past there's been this kind of stigma around 'vanity publishing'. The sense that somehow it makes you a lesser writer. But I think that's nonsense, and actually it pays really good royalties. Like up to 70%, in comparison with the usual 10. And previously, if you self-published, you had to print your pamphlets yourself, and distribute them your-self, which is time-consuming and expensive. But now, through the digital store, you can reach a really big audience for free, or relatively little. Some of the most successful cases have sold millions of copies.

P: How would you find out about one of those books, without it being marketed by a big house?

L: Through customer reviews and ratings.

P: Does that mean you've had a pile of competition entries to read between rehearsals? Is that not a bit of a chore?

L: Oh, I only have to read the final shortlist. And I'm quite excit-ed to see them — hopefully there will be some gems.

P: It sounds like you rarely buy printed publications.

L: Not at all! I picked up a few at Word on the Water only the other day. It's moored at Granary Square by Central Saint Martins right now.

P: Is that the bookshop on a narrow boat?
    L: Yeah, it looked so sweet so I went in.

P: Did you buy anything?
    L: I got something for myself and a couple of books for my daughter, Wylde. She loves books, it makes me very happy. We've amassed a great collection of kids' books. Tea gave us some great ones, actually. When Wylde was first born, she gave us a Yayoi Kusama version of *Alice's Adventures in Wonderland* and The Brothers Grimm... We taught our daughter sign language early on and though she still can't say the word 'book', she's not afraid to clap when she wants one...

P: Is a clap sign language for 'book'?
    L: Yes!

P: You'd better watch that, she'll be at it like those cats on Instagram with the dinner bell. You've made a rod for your own back there.
    L: She does get really upset if you don't go and get her one down from the bookcase when she claps. She tears them up as well — it's not like she has the utmost respect for them as objects yet. So having her has certainly kept me shopping for physical books. I think it's fair to say that most books I read make their way to me mysteriously, somehow, but the ones I buy from bookshops are mostly gifts for other people.

P: In these days when libraries are closing around us, a knowledgeable bookshop keeper can be as valuable as a senior reference librarian.
    L: Lucy Moore at Claire de Rouen is amazing. I'll text her, email her or call her and be like, 'Hey, I've got to buy this present for this person' and she goes, 'OK, what are they like? What kind of things are they interested in?' Then she spends time looking and will text me five recommendations to choose from. It's great, isn't it? She does that for lots of customers, I think.

11. DINNER BELL

A reliable method for acquiring fleeting fame is to record a cat being cute in a hitherto undreamt-of way then to post the video online as per the Oregon scientists who trained cats to ring dinner bells in order to receive tasty treats.

P: Did you see that piece Michiko Kakutani re-tweeted the other day, about the five things that bookshop owners hate most? The one that really broke my heart was when people come in, use that expert service, find the perfect thing and then tell the shopkeeper, 'Oh, thanks, I'll get it on Amazon.'
    L: That's awful! Who would do that? Why would they do that? I buy lots of things on Amazon, I'm ashamed to say.

12. JEFF BEZOS
—
The Amazon founder's side projects include a gigantic clock inside a Texan mountain. Once built, the Clock of the Long Now will tick once per year, for at least 10,000 years.

P: Why ashamed? Because you think Jeff Bezos is a terrible man?

L: No, I just think that it's nice to support independent publishing and independent bookshops. But on so many practical levels, it's so much easier to buy books on Amazon.

P: Well, there's your answer. Are you particular about how you store your books?

L: No. There's a colour-coded bookshelf in the play — you'll see it tonight — which I thought was nice, but at home in King's Cross ours are all over the place. I've got too many, probably. When I was making my list for you, I was looking at them all and thinking, 'So many of these I've already read or I have no interest in reading.' I should edit them.

P: I always liked what the guitarist John Squire said in an interview when asked if his record collection was as good as Bobby Gillespie's. He said, 'I've still got all my mistakes.' If collections are biographical, where the bad plays as important a part as the good, I wonder if editing them risks revising one's life story. Or at least the story of your intellectual life.

L: It's true that the history of my reading has been a sort of continuum that paralleled whatever I was doing at the time.

P: Did modelling interrupt that continuum?

L: I don't think so; I was reading just as avidly in those days. Though I started modelling when I was fourteen, I stayed in school until I was eighteen. And probably the height of my modelling career was when I was fifteen, sixteen, seventeen. So by the time my history and politics teacher encouraged me to apply to Cambridge during A levels, it was perfectly possible for me to imagine the two working together simultaneously. The teacher used to write me these very witty, lovely letters, which I've lost, I think. I wish I hadn't...

P: They'll probably turn up in a textbook.

L: Probably some day. I hadn't been sure whether to apply; I thought maybe it was better to just go off and work, but he wrote me a long letter detailing why I should at least try, so I had a choice. I applied to read Art History, got in and then was on the horns of a dilemma for two years. I deferred twice.

P: The fashion world can feel like a very sunny place when things are going well.

L: It wasn't even just fashion; I started doing films in those two years: I did *St Trinian's*, then *Doctor Parnassus*, and then *Rage* by

Sally Potter, back to back. Sometimes I look back and I think, God! I should've just gone with that, because going to my agents, 'All right, I'll see you in three years!' interrupted that impetus. But truth be told, in the three years that I was in Cambridge I read a bunch of scripts, and the only one I thought I would quit university for was Steve McQueen's *Shame*.

P: That screenplay was written by Abi Morgan, I think.

L: But by the time I'd read it, they'd actually already offered Carey Mulligan the part. Off the record.

P: Really, why off the record?

L: Well, I suppose it doesn't matter; it was an amazing script.

P: You got a double first from King's, didn't you? You must have worked your ass off.

L: Yes, I'd love to pretend that I was super-lazy and I'm just a genius, but no, I worked very hard in the final stages. Most of the year I was in and out of university, working and doing real life, but in the final month of each year I just stopped, locked myself in a hole and focused. I was always quite academically interested. When I'm interested in what I'm doing I become a bit obsessive-compulsive.

P: Did your degree change anything for you?

L: Of course, everything changes your life, right? I think it changed the way I see the world.

P: And perhaps the way the world sees you. If I think back to when I first started working in fashion at the start of the noughties, I was really struck by how many models and creatives — particularly the hair and make-up artists — would have a fashionable book displayed prominently at the top of their bags.

L: That's true — fashion people are big readers. I mean, doesn't everyone read a lot?

P: I don't think everyone does, though. And I have to admit that initially I wondered whether those people were all protesting too much — that it was a sort of pre-emptive strike against anyone who might presume that we're all dummies in the fashion industry, only interested in flimflam and parties.

L: Ha, well, that's partly true but we also like a good book!

P: You say you're really good at focusing on one thing and yet your career is so broad. Was it always the plan to have such a varied portfolio?

L: I never had a plan, no. I just follow my interests and it happens to be that they're quite varied. They're all quite geeky: either arty, creative stuff, or kind of political, social stuff. Fashion lies outside both those two camps, but then fashion was just accidental.

P: And supportive.

L: True, modelling has been hugely enabling.

P: Do you ever feel like you have to defend the multifarious nature of your career? The British press don't like anyone who's too clever or too good at too many things.

L: Yes, people do love labelling people, pigeonholing them. I don't read too much of what's written about me, but I feel like it's been pretty positive on the whole. Especially when I was in university, the narrative was always very positive and encouraging, as opposed to belittling. It's quite hard to find an argument against someone wanting to educate themselves.

P: You might say what unites your many different projects is that they are all idealistic, in the very best possible sense of the word.

L: Maybe, yes. There's an Oscar Wilde quote that utopia is an island for which man sets sail and, upon reaching it, sets sail again. So I'd say yes, a lot of what I do probably does have a utopian spirit behind it. But none of it's saying, 'This is the perfect solution.'

PENNY MARTIN is Editor-in-chief of The *Gentlewoman* magazine — sister magazine to *The Happy Reader* and its brother, *Fantastic Man*. Like Lily, she has had numerous other titles, including Chair (of fashion imagery at London College of Fashion), Curator (of collections at The Fawcett Library) and Gallery Assistant (at Glasgow Museums). Her first job was also in theatre, however, working as a dresser on a 1989 repertory production of *When the Wind Blows*.

Cole's apartment is enviably close to the British Library, which by law receives every book published in the UK. Hair: Kei Terada at Julian Watson Agency. Make up: Siddhartha Simone at Julian Watson Agency.

UTOPIAN READS

As you might imagine, Lily's reading list is packed with idealism and pep.

ADA OR ARDOR: A FAMILY CHRONICLE (1969)
Vladimir Nabokov

When Lily is asked to name favourite book, she tends to say *Ada or Arbor*. Nabokov's longest novel, a much less famous work than *Lolita* or *Pale Fire*, tells the story of a troubled love affair between a man named Van Veen and a woman — his direct relation — named Ada. More than that, it's an elaborate examination of the nature of happiness and the essence of time. It's a book that Lily reads 'perpetually'.

NINE STORIES (1953)
J.D. Salinger

From this seminal collection by the American master, Lily points specifically to 'Teddy', a story that smuggles in various tenets of Buddhist and Hindu philosophy via the story of a ten-year-old child on a luxury liner. Why this story in particular? Because, says Lily, it is 'disturbing and poetic and spiritually arresting all at the same time'.

THE ARGONAUTS (2015)
Maggie Nelson

The story of Maggie Nelson's relationship with her partner, the fluidly gendered artist Harry Dodge. Maggie weaves autobiography and gender theory together in a watery narrative that spills across time, thoughts and the experience of love. Gender and cultural theorists, the 'many-gendered mothers' of our narrator's heart, act as a kind of encouraging Greek chorus, their words in the margins guiding Maggie as she navigates this new emotional terrain.

FOR-GIVING (1997)
Genevieve Vaughan

True to its own subject matter, *For-Giving* is available online for free. Says Lily: 'The ideas offer a paradigm shift as far as I'm concerned. Vaughan argues that exchange paradigms (for example barter, or more explicitly money and capitalism) are a consequence of patriarchy, whereas gifting is a feminist principle because it is rooted in the experience of mothering (i.e. you give to your child without any expectation of return). I think that principle can (and should) be applied to fathering too.'

THE SOCIETY OF THE SPECTACLE (1967)
Guy Debord

'All that was once directly lived has become mere representation,' wrote French writer and film-maker Guy Debord. He was talking about life in the 1960s, but that statement has just become truer and truer. The reader can do nothing but put the book down and mutter, 'Wow, how did he know?' before sharing the quote online.

HEART OF DARKNESS (1899)
Joseph Conrad

As timeless classics go, *Heart of Darkness* inhabits an uneasy and much-debated position. Tracing a hallucinatory boat journey inland up the Congo River in search of a man named Kurtz (a wayward employee of the so-called 'Company'), Conrad's claustrophobic masterpiece has been alternately hailed as an early indictment of empire and condemned for its outdated racial attitudes.

WALDEN (1854)
Henry David Thoreau

'I went to the woods because I wished to live deliberately, to front only the essential facts of life.' This desire to cast off the shackles of an industrialised life to search for deeper meaning has travelled a long way from Thoreau's account of his experience of isolation in the Massachusetts woods in 1854.

THE ENCHANTER (2011)
Lila Azam Zanganeh

A blend of fiction and essays based on Zanganeh's lifelong love of Nabokov (and her close friendship with his son, Dmitri) results in a book that is completely uncategorisable. If, upon reading Nabokov, you have ever felt something approaching a transcendental experience, this book will bring those memories swirling gloriously back to you. And, if not: read this to understand why so many worship him.

THE GIFT (1983)
Lewis Hyde

What role exactly does the gift play in our market-driven economy? So asked the cultural critic Lewis Hyde in a book that Lily describes as tracing the 'anthropological history of gift cultures' and which provided inspiration for the gift economy of Impossible, her online sharing platform.

WUTHERING HEIGHTS (1847)
Emily Brontë

Love, death and snowstorms: everyone likes *Wuthering Heights*, surely. In fact the book met with mixed reviews on publication, which seems extraordinary given the now-canonical status of Emily Brontë's wiley, windy — and only — novel.

THE HAPPY
READER

Precious metal rectangles, swigs of grog and smooth-tongued chefs with portable parrots: part two of The Happy Reader is beached on the shores of TREASURE ISLAND, the unbelievably famous story by Robert Louis Stevenson.

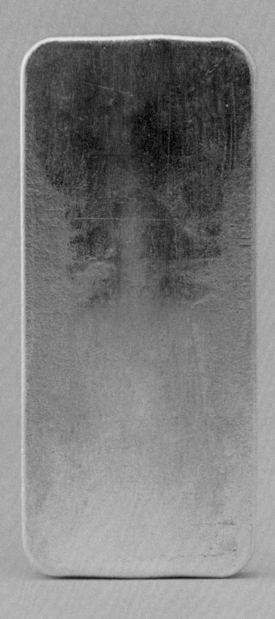

ARTEFACT
It all starts with a dead man's chest, that of deceased pirate Billy Bones, whose belongings include 'several sticks of tobacco, two brace of very handsome pistols, a piece of bar silver, an old Spanish watch and some other trinkets of little value.' Here a piece of bar silver kindly loaned to us by Baird & Co Bullion Merchants, London, is photographed by IVAN RUBERTO. For more from Ivan's piratical series of still-life images see pages 33, 52 and 60.

Amid all the inflatable whatnots and naked people waiting for ice cream, most summer seasides show clear visual echoes of a novel named *Treasure Island*. SEB EMINA introduces our current communal read — the Book of the Season — an adventure story that's so omnipresent one forgets what a thrilling tale it is.

TREASURE EVERYWHERE

In the city of Treasure Island, Florida, police officers wear badges depicting a bearded, cutlass-wielding pirate standing over a chest of treasure. Behind this bearded outlaw are — *quelle surprise* — a beach, a tree, the sea and a distant ship. That a traffic offender who glances at this badge will be momentarily transported to a parallel universe of swash-buckling nautical adventures is mostly thanks to a book written once upon a time by a sickly Scottish man in a kind of trance.

In 1881, Robert Louis Stevenson — whose later novels would include *The Strange Case of Dr Jekyll and Mr Hyde* — drew a treasure map to entertain his stepson. As Stevenson gazed at this map, a story began unfurling in his mind, its essential components arriving in such a fully formed state that it was as if the story was not so much composed as discovered.

A boy named Jim Hawkins is working in his parents' inn when a roguish, shanty-lovin' guest dies, leaving behind a chest containing all the typical junk that every retired pirate accu-mulates but also... a treasure map. A danger-ous sea voyage ensues, involving a one-legged ship's cook, a half-crazed castaway, a band of rum-swilling pirates, a skeleton that doubles as a signpost, several battles involving excruciat-ingly slow firearms, and, of course, an island.

Jim calls it Treasure Island, despite the dead pirate referring to it as Skeleton Island. Treasure Island in Florida gained its name after a hotel owner buried and then 'discov-ered' wooden chests on the local beaches. It's just as well Robert Louis Stevenson didn't stick to his original title, *The Sea Cook*; that would not be a good name for a city. When it comes to branding, *Treasure Island* is probably the most effective pair of words ever placed next to one another. Treasure Island Mall is

a shopping destination in Madhya Pradesh, India. Treasure Island Media is one of the world's oldest gay-porn production companies. Treasure Island Music Festival (named after an also-eponymous artificial island in San Francisco Bay) will take place on the week-end of 14 and 15 October. Treasure Island is a casino in Las Vegas and a chain of storage facilities in and around New York City.

It's a great title for a book, too. Among other things, this is because it'd be the correct answer if someone held a gun to your head and shouted, 'Condense the story into two words!' Is this why so many people who haven't read it talk about it as if they have? Or is that down to the many thousands of times the book has been adapted into plays, movies, video games and so on? The conventions that were so effectively arranged — if not always originally conceived of — in Stevenson's novel, from the parroty squawk of 'pieces of eight!' to the very trope of a treasure map itself, are so common-place now that the act of actually reading the book can seem almost a waste of time.

But it's a shame if we feel this way. En-countered in their original setting, these clichés are no longer clichés at all but are as fresh as the spray of the sea as it collides with a bloodstained rock. The language has a rollicking tempo, subtlety and wit, and encountered in his original setting, Long John Silver is not a hackneyed panto stalwart but a work of vivid genius. If

you look carefully, you can find hints of class politics (what is a ship but a microcosm of society?), imperial angst (where did this 'treasure' come from exactly?) and just about any ancient story involving a boy who leaves home on a dangerous journey and returns a man (a later equivalent is *Star Wars*).

As Stevenson wrote *Treasure Island*, he read his efforts out loud to his family, day by day, chapter by chapter: his elderly father was as thrilled and impatient as his stepson. The novel is still appreciated by everyone from newly literate children to heavyweight critics. The latter call him 'RLS' — and RLS succumbed to his long-standing health problems ten years later, by which point he, his wife and stepchildren had relocated to the Samoan island of Upolo. He died aged just forty-four. *Treasure Island* is 136 and counting. It has never been, and will never be, out of print. For evidence of its never-ending influence, go to any town with a vague seafaring heritage. Are the knick-knacks on offer in the tourist shops based on the navy, or on pirates?

NIGHTLIFE

The Admiral Benbow is a shipwreck-themed pub in the town of Penzance, Cornwall. JEREMY ALLEN, a lapsed regular, recalls a place of outlandish rumours infused with the threat of minor acts of violence.

DOWN THE PUB

Like any sane adult I have an aversion to theme pubs, and yet a public house with a nautical *mise-en-scène* was the one I cut my teeth in. The Admiral Benbow in Penzance is an inscrutable bolthole that's a cut above your common-or-garden theme bar. The lounge brims with Jacobean mastheads, ship wheels, sailing knots and cannons, while tall punters risk decapitation from the low-flying beams. Many will know the Admiral Benbow's name from *Treasure Island*, and plenty assume the Cornish boozer is the one in the book, probably conflating Robert Louis Stevenson with Gilbert and Sullivan. Shropshire also has an Admiral Benbow, and so too does Lisburn in County Antrim, though neither of them are the real thing either (the pub in the novel, named after naval officer John Benbow, is fictional).

Getting served at the pub on Chapel Street, one of Cornwall's most historic thoroughfares, was a rite of passage for many a strapling in the early 1990s. Back then it was all too easy to imagine oneself on the hull of a ship, three sheets to the wind. Especially on Saturday nights, when teens lurched from side to side and occasionally threw up in the corner. It was like *The Raft of the Medusa*, with dehydration at the bar, mutiny at the pool table and outbreaks of scurvy over at the fruit machine. I never thought much about where the maritime miscellany had appeared from; it's not something that troubles you when sneaking nervously into a back room awaiting an elicit pint of scrumpy to hold in both hands, brought to you by your most grown-up-looking friend.

Covert attendance eventually transmogrified into preening territorially around the pool table, the cynosure of the back room. Even strangers would grudgingly watch as you clattered red and yellow spheres around the green baize, lit from above. Before there was portable technology to get lost in, your objective would be to get on and then stay on the table for as long as possible without getting deposed.

1. GILBERT AND SULLIVAN

—

In 1897, composer Arthur Sullivan and lyricist William Schwenck Gilbert chose Penzance as the setting of their two-act opera *The Pirates of Penzance*. The opera remains popular to this day, spawning several revivals, a Tony Award winning stint on Broadway, a film adaptation starring Kevin Kline and Angela Lansbury, and a 2014 staging at Penzance's beloved Penlee Park Open Air Theatre

2. PELAGIC FOLKLORE
—
The term pelagic pertains to open water that is neither close to the bottom nor near to the shore, a mysterious zone that has inspired countless myths and folk-tales. A Cornish example is the Mermaid of Padstow, who conjured a great storm after being shot by a fisherman who'd mistaken her for a seal.

I would hang on for several hours sometimes, at least if Darren Hardman — the town psychopath — didn't show up.

If the audience soon lost interest in your ephemeral celebrity, the haunted wooden masthead carved into the shape of a lady would keep staring. One presumes she continued to stare even after the drunks had been kicked out and the lights switched off. She's been staring for centuries now, and it's probably for the best that she can't relate the horrors she's witnessed.

Like all the best pubs, the Admiral Benbow is said to be haunted, by Annabella or Arabella — nobody's sure which — who laments for a love lost at sea... or so the story goes. To add to the pelagic folklore, an article recently appeared in an untrustworthy national newspaper about a smuggler's tunnel leading from the harbour up to the inn. It should be taken with a pinch of salt. 'Every time the Benbow has new owners you can guarantee that a paper somewhere will run with the "discovery" of yet another bloody tunnel,' one angry local told me, suggesting it might be a ruse to cook up some free advertising. 'I admit that they appear to have found something. But *really*? A smuggler's tunnel?'

The building was first converted from cottages into a coffee house in the 1950s by local seadog Roland Morris, who showcased exotic blends from around the world. It was clearly decades ahead of its time; Penzance wasn't quite ready for a proto-hipster coffee joint just yet. It then opened as the Admiral Benbow pub in 1956, complete with Octavius Lanyon — a distinctive gun-wielding life-size figure — lying prostrate on top of the roof.

Morris, who could be described as Penzance's last pirate, filled the interior with objects he'd recovered from the HMS *Association*, which went down off the Isles of Scilly on 22 October 1707. The booty that Morris salvaged some two and a half centuries later was bountiful, with much of what was taken from the seabed ending up in the Roland Morris Maritime Museum in Penzance. What didn't go on display went to auction, making the buccaneer a pretty penny.

The National Trust invoked an ancient fifteenth-century law to try to force Morris to give up the location of the HMS *Association* and

A drawing of the Admiral Benbow by the pub's original landlord Roland Morris.

the other boats that sunk that night, but he wasn't the kind of man to genuflect to authority. The scallywag still appeared to be evading them when the Yorkshire TV documentary *The Sea Always Wins* was shown on terrestrial television in 1982, though he did suggest he would cough up the information eventually. The *Association* was one of four ships that went down on that fateful eighteenth-century night, and Morris appeared to know where all the wrecks were resting. In what was one of Britain's most catastrophic naval disasters, more than 1,500 sailors lost their lives.

I was nearly done for myself the night the aforementioned Darren Hardman came into the pub. Darren was on Pubwatch, meaning he was barred from every drinking establishment in town. That didn't stop him entering the back room and brazenly sinking the black ball into a pocket with his hand, rendering the game I was playing over. A titter resounded from his giant chest. Instinctively and furiously, I marched over in order to confront him, although once I squared up to him I soon became pain-fully aware of my own shortfall. That evening I discovered what Dutch courage is all about. In the weediest of voices, which took on a trembly, vertiginous pitch, I uttered the words, 'You're a wanker.'

A hush descended on the room. A whole minute seemed to elapse. Spectators waited to see what the notorious Mr Hardman would do. He gazed down upon me and grimaced. In an instant, he wafted his gigantic arm through the air and clasped his mighty hand around my throat. As he compressed my neck with his thumb and finger, my feet briefly left the floor. But instead of asphyxiating me for long, he let out a roar of ap-preciation, dropped me back onto my feet and then promptly left again.

Years have passed since the great Benbow strangling incident, and it's only in recent times that I've learned to keep my mouth shut by staying sober. In the intervening period I appear to have lost all interest in pool, while Darren has spent much of his time at Her Majesty's pleasure. The Benbow, meanwhile, is still open for business down-stairs, but the phantasmagorical upper level can be frequented only as a room-for-hire for special events.

JEREMY ALLEN writes for the *Guardian*, the BBC, the *Quietus*, etc. His favourite island is Sicily for its scary hairpin bends, vertiginous alpine residences and Paler-mo's gritty charm and ugly Frankenstein cathedral.

MUSIC

So long as others sing along, a sailor loves to sing a song. DANIEL RACHEL gains a rare interview with former XTC frontman ANDY PARTRIDGE about the special alchemy of music you can join in with.

WHY AREN'T YOU SINGING?

When Andy Partridge hears a chord played on a guitar, or a little musical phrase, he paints an immediate picture in his head. He says, 'It's like painting the scenery in a stage production.' Synaesthesia is a condition few other songwriters share. Partridge is best known as the frontman of XTC, whose hits include 'Making Plans for Nigel' and 'Sgt Rock (Is Going to Help Me)', but perhaps the band's best-loved song, 'Senses Working Over-time', began by fortune. Partridge intended to play a major chord on his acoustic guitar

RLS

Robert Louis Stevenson (1850–1894) was born in Edinburgh and died in Vailima, a village in the Pacific nation of Samoa. Between these two events he travelled widely and wrote a large number of books including *The Strange Case of Dr Jekyll and Mr Hyde*, *Kidnapped* and *Travels with a Donkey in the Cévennes*. Stevenson's final home in Vailima has been preserved as a museum; the author himself is buried atop a nearby mountain.

Giving it all you've got is mostly fun when everyone else is doing so too.

but accidentally struck two dissonant notes. Inspired by their unfamiliarity, he imagined 'some medieval serf ploughing... like a little picture in an illustrated Bible'. He began to describe the scene in his mind's eye, and then later, by piecing together two other existing ideas, the song was completed and resulted in the group's first Top Ten hit, a record with preternaturally sing-alongable qualities.

D: Could you define what a singalong song is?

A: Blimey! It helps if it's in your own language. Although one can pick up a really moronic song in another language in seconds, which doesn't mean it can't be astute and observant. A lot of nursery rhymes for example were political commentary. I would suggest the nursery rhyme is the godfather of singalong songs.

D: Nursery rhyme is interesting, because I was thinking of 'Yellow Submarine' as a benchmark of a singalong.

A: As benchmarks you'd have things like 'The Birdie Song' or 'Agadoo', push pineapple, shake the tree. Loathe them or hate them, singalong songs do serve a purpose — they help to kill off old folk while they attempt to dance around to one.

D: Is the importance of a singalong first and foremost melody?

A: No, given a football crowd's propensity for singing everything horrendously out of tune. It's probably a combination of tribal rhythm and melody. The biggest football singalong of all time was that clapping pattern which usually ends with the club's name.

D: 'Senses Working Overtime' came about when you set out to write the most 'instantly moronic' chorus you could think of, by reversing Manfred Mann's '5-4-3-2-1'.

A: Yes. Counting is one of the first things we learn to do as kids. So I thought, 'Why not tap into that.' I also tried it with 'Statue of Liberty' with the woh oh oh melody. I remember one specific gig in Blackpool when the power went down. 'Oh, that's just perfect!' But the audience carried on. I was conducting it, bellowing *a cappella* from the stage, and they were all singing along. It made it an event.

D: Have you been embroiled in singalongs?

A: Oh, yeah, hundreds of times. Drunken lock-ins, in pubs, where you end up singing rugby songs. It's best if alcoholically fuelled, because it removes any self-awareness of making a berk of yourself. Large crowds can do that because one's IQ diminishes the more people that are around you; one trims one's wit to suit.

D: You used to fight your audience at gigs.

A: It was that Pete Townshend thing, 'Pretend you're in a war.' It's you against the audience. I would secretly despise audiences who sang along to the chorus. When we did 'Helicopter', which is a very silly song, everyone would suddenly leap to their feet or rush to the front, and part of me would be thinking, 'Idiots. Why didn't you rush to the front when we were playing something a bit more obscure?'

D: You were after greater appreciation.

A: Playing live was just: get through the set in one piece, get to bed and on to the next town. It was about survival. The last time that happened I was in a pub in Bath with a dozen or so people around me. I did a Q&A at a bookshop, and after about a dozen people followed me to a pub where a friend of mine had brought his guitar along. I made a drunken fist of playing some old XTC numbers and felt very uncomfortable doing it.

D: The ideal scenario being the singalong but without you at the centre, orchestrating.

A: I would find nothing weird about being an observer in the corner with a stuck-on beard just looking how it was all going and nobody knowing who the hell I was. I like to be the back-room boy.

D: Can you divorce yourself and see the song as the centre of attention?

A: Definitely. Once you've written the song, you then kick it out of home: 'You're big enough and hairy arsed enough to make your own way. Go.' Art is never finished; it's only ever abandoned. Get shot of it. Move on to the next thing. You go from creating this musical child to then despising it and wanting it out of the house. You haven't got space for any more musical children if the place is full up with the old ones.

DANIEL RACHEL's books include *Isle of Noises: Conversations with Great British Songwriters* and *Walls Come Tumbling Down: the music and politics of Rock Against Racism, 2 Tone and Red Wedge.*

FIRST TIME

The Jamaican poet ISHION HUTCHINSON loves *Treasure Island* because it reminds him of home. Not that the landscape is Caribbean — it isn't — but because it works as both time machine and transportation device, to a certain chair in a certain house, a very long time ago.

TALES FROM A READER

The books we love look over us. One leans closest to me always and with an angel's aura. It draws me up into its radiance. The radiance is childhood, not adolescence — that province *Treasure Island* makes eternal, brilliant as shoals at night.

If a true classic is, as the French critic Charles Augustin Sainte-Beuve put it, what 'has enriched the human mind, increased its treasure', then *Treasure Island* is the storehouse I find fresh joy in on every return. I first opened it in a lattice chair on my grandma's veranda in Port Antonio, Jamaica. The years revolve and it has ceased being a book. I think of it as a place, not quite home, but one which fills me with the sensation of home, calm exhilaration. Far away from home, I have stalked out many times into strange cities to find a copy: I found it in Berlin once during a rainstorm day. Another time was in Marrakech, hours of entering riads hoping a tourist might have left a copy behind, only to find one inside a stationery shop. Reading *Treasure Island* in these distant places was a way to moor myself back to what I knew — the sea — in order to immerse myself, with greater confidence, into what I did not know.

For its true element is a sea I can recall with vernacular force. Though this sea does not appear in Stevenson's book and could not have either, the prose has magnified its tattered presence, scrolling and unscrolling, beyond all I saw looking down from my grandmother's hill to Port Antonio and the dense green of Fort George peninsula. In that greenness, my school. Built from the bowels of a British fort, Titchfield High resembled drained khaki-sentinels teetering on the edge of the water. But either history or desperation kept them from falling over. Of course, I would not have perceived them in this language at this time. A lone surveyor of the open sea, what I lacked then as a boy was the trust of naming what was mine. The need to sound the names of the bays, the coves, the ridges fading behind our house, was unbearable.

Names exist for them and they are beautiful but cruel. Herein lies the great Caribbean hurt, all the names of everything in my reality derived from colonial subjugation. It takes a certain cosmic or psychic courage to say their names — Frenchman's Cove, Blue Lagoon — without self-betrayal. Thus, my breath caught at the start of *Treasure Island* when Jim Hawkins declares, as his purpose for writing about the island, 'because there is still treasure [there] not yet lifted'.

The fettering of 'there is' to 'not yet' expresses the essential — the existential — post-colonial contradiction, that air of dispossession which never disappears, which even owning a land title scarcely salves. This was the eternal worry of my grandmother, a baker who sold in the Musgrave Market, who could only make a shaky X in the signature line of her property deed, giving her life's work a pirate's marker, fully aware she has not named herself or anything else. Her eyes held an injured and assaulted stare whenever we visited the Registry of Deeds Office. And it was for this very reason I felt a subtle kinship with Hawkins as I read and she passed me with a bushel of my white school shirts, quiet to not distract me from the pages.

Like boy me, Jim Hawkins was a pirate of circumstance, an outlaw forced to be 'a good, prompt subaltern', up against the torrents of life. Even so, he still expressed the long vision to claim a possibility to come. He himself was that possibility, which was also the way my grandmother saw me, silently affirming in me a future neither of us were able to judge. So, I claimed him.

The claim was of moral dignity. Fiction's vision-clearing power let me see through the colonial degradation and the leftover poverty of our rural coastal town, long stretches of blighted coconut trees resembling an outpost of progress, only with expensive tourist oases hidden in the Blue Mountain range and villas nested in the coves near the beaches.

What I read in *Treasure Island* blazed with strange familiarity. The prose reflected all I saw around me, not in terms of description but within the sinew of the language, its skipping stone weighted with Melville's idea that true places never are down in any map. A map was not necessary to live 'the joy of exploration', as Jim Hawkins says. In fact, as soon as he gets to the island he abandons the security of the map, trusting to his sharp 'weather-eye' intuition to guide him through the unknown. The story is most dramatically intense in those moments; both because of the natural threats — what predators are in the bushes? — and the drunk, murdering pirates hunting him.

3. TREASURE ISLAND

—

There is always a stage adaptation of *Treasure Island* taking place somewhere in the world, and usually there are several. For example, right now you could see it at:
- Stratford Festival (Ontario, Canada) Until 2 October
- Sidekick Theatre (Minneapolis, USA) 21 June – 29 July
- Dukes Outdoor Theatre (Lancaster, UK) 4 July – 12 August
- Utah Shakespeare Festival (Cedar City, USA) 5 July – 2 September
- Mount Baker Theatre (Bellingham, USA) 15 July
- Walking Theatre Company (Selkirk, UK) 27 July
- Minack Theatre (Penzance, UK) 7 – 11 August

ISLAND OF THE IMPOSSIBLE
Many expect the scenery of *Treasure Island* to be Caribbean but it is in fact based on the wilds of continental North America, and specifically the Californian wilderness. Here, the work of Californian artist-photographer DAVID BENJAMIN SHERRY offers visions more of a piece with the hallucinatory nature of Stevenson's work than any mere beach-plus-palm-tree.

LEE SHORE
Somehow, in *Treasure Island*, the unreal landscapes, like no island on Earth, make the scenic setting much more timeless than it would be otherwise, taking the reader on a unique and other-worldly trip into the unknown.

DEEP WATER
Robert Louis Stevenson travelled to California in 1879 to visit Fanny Van de Grift Osbourne, a married woman he had met and befriended while visiting Paris. She left her husband, and they married in San Francisco.

Yet, often, these moments coincide with serene instances of revelation, very similar to the physical melody I experienced daily when walking the beach inlet of Bryan's Bay. Our islands touched and blurred; Hawkins and I became spirit companions:

> As I continued to thread the tall woods, I could hear from far before me not only the continuous thunder of the surf, but a certain tossing of foliage and grinding of boughs which showed me the sea breeze had set in higher than usual. Soon cool draughts of air began to reach me, and a few steps farther I came forth into the open borders of the grove, and saw the sea lying blue and sunny to the horizon and the surf tumbling and tossing its foam along the beach.

The 'certain tossing of foliage' I would have heard were the leaves of the sea grape trees, and it was below their shades I first finished the book. On the hill behind me was my grandmother's yellow house, in front of me was the sea and floating on it was the spectral blue-green of Navy Island. 'Not a man, not a sail, upon the sea; the very largeness of the view increased the sense of solitude.'

Stevenson writes like an eavesdropper on my heart.

ISHION HUTCHINSON was born in Port Antonio, Jamaica. His most recent poetry collection is titled *House of Lords and Commons*. He dedicates this piece to the wonderfully-named Pyrate Jacob Chen, a friend's son whom he gave a copy of RLS's novel some years ago.

GLOSSARY

Everybody these days thinks they can chat like a lawless old salt. Just go 'arrrr' and 'me lad' a lot, and the effect is achieved, is it not? Then we read *Treasure Island*: a vast menagerie of archaic terms with precise technical meanings. Our bluff is called. JEAN HANNAH EDELSTEIN compiles a short glossary to put the aspiring sea-thief back on course.

DIFFICULT WORD LIST

ABEAM — At a right angle to your boat. You might say, 'Ship abeam!' or 'Killer whale abeam!' or 'Coastguard abeam!' if you're really in trouble.

AVAST — You'd then cry 'Avast!' to the coastguard, because that means 'Hold it right there!'

BELAY — You will be familiar with this word if you were into rock climbing before you decided to get into pirating instead. In your new hobby it is a way to tell somebody to cut it out.

BREECHES — Those are your trousers if you're a British pirate, or your pants if you're an American one. They fasten above your knee, to avoid soggy cuffs.

CAREEN — When you need to clean your ship you turn it on its side and you tell your pals: 'I'm careening the ship!' They should disembark first.

DADDLE — To pull one over on someone, such as a lubber, which is a person who probably suffers from seasickness and therefore deserves to be swindled.

HO — An exclamation, often accompanied by 'Hey!'

KEELHAULING — Dragging someone under your boat as a punishment. These days, legally speaking, this is probably better applied as a threat rather than as an active form of torture.

MATEY — Who's your mate? Now that you're a pirate, they're your matey. Can be usefully hostile when delivered to a matey with a touch of sneer.

PANNIKIN — Cup, made of metal, from which you sup liquids: your ale, your cider, or your scurvy-beating tonic water.

QUARTER — That's where you hang out: your space on the boat. If you give no quarter, it means that you're not going to take any prisoners, which is to say that you're not going to bang them up in your ship, or, God forbid, threaten to keelhaul them, you monster.

SCUPPERS — That's a hole in your boat deck, to drain water. Not a hole that sinks your boat. It's important to know the difference.

JEAN HANNAH EDELSTEIN is a Brooklyn-based writer who spent three nights at Treasure Island Hotel & Casino, Las Vegas on a press trip in 2009. She'll write about this formative experience in detail in her forthcoming book, *This Really Isn't About You* (Picador, 2018).

POLITICS

Who on earth could have predicted the rise of the pirate politician? AMELIA TAIT speaks to the leaders of a surprisingly popular movement that could only have sprung up in our technology-ridden era.

THREE CHEERS FOR PIRACY

If, at any point after July 2004, you have sat down to watch a movie, then it is likely that you've been confidently told, 'You wouldn't steal a car.' These words were prominently featured in a now infamous anti-piracy ad that — despite your best efforts — would staunchly refuse to respond to your DVD player's 'Skip' button.

'You wouldn't steal a handbag,' goes the clip, as a girl downloads a movie in her bedroom. 'You wouldn't steal a television.' When the teen cancels her download, four words shake somewhat comically across the screen: 'Piracy. It's a crime.'

It's safe to say this video did little to discourage a generation of teenagers from streaming, torrenting and downloading music, movies and TV shows for free from the shadowy universe of websites that offer such services. Yet, although most don't see this behaviour as equivalent to stealing a car, the word 'pirate' undeniably still carries some residual stigma.

Add the word 'party' and this stigma is softened — but only because it conjures up images of a child waving a plastic sword to celebrate their tenth birthday.

'Yeah, every day,' laughs David Elston, the leader of the Pirate Party UK (PPUK), when I ask if he ever considers changing the party's name. PPUK is one of over forty political pirate parties that have sprung up across the world in the last decade, occasionally with startling levels of electoral success. Although, as the name suggests, these parties were born out of a preoccupation with copyright laws, their policies focus on a multitude of issues surrounding the modern, digital world.

'It's thrown around as an insult, but really, when you think about it, it's actually a very good thing,' says Elston. 'You want a free culture and you don't want people dying because of drug patents. You want to protect free speech, and you want to be able to live your life in private without government snooping... if that's what a pirate is, then call me a pirate.'

Yet the man who started it all can undeniably be seen online, wearing an eyepatch.

'I bought five of them in a pharmacy; it's actually a medical eyepatch,' says Rick Falkvinge, founder of the first ever Pirate Party, in Sweden. Born Dick Greger Augustsson, Falkvinge changed his name to mean 'Falconwing' in 2004 to symbolise his attitude to freedom.

'It's a fine line to walk when you have a name like the Pirate Party in terms of just how much can you play on it before it goes overboard and becomes clowning,' he says. 'So I figured that standing in a three-piece suit outside the European Parliament looking into the distance with a solemn face and wearing one eyepatch would be how far I would go.'

Generally, Falkvinge is a serious man. When he speaks about the Pirate Party, which he founded in 2006 after the unauthorised sharing of copyrighted material was criminalised in Sweden, he does so with a breathless urgency. 'Politicians did not understand the reality of people working, living, socialising online,' he says.

Though 'piracy' originally described theft at sea, it has a surprisingly long history in relation to intellectual property: as early as 1603, the playwright Thomas Dekker called plagiarists 'word-pirates'. Falkvinge points out the long history of what he calls the 'copyright lobby', stating that they attempted to prevent the establishment of UK public libraries in 1849. 'They said that you can't possibly allow everybody to read any book for free. Nobody would be able to make a living as an author. Nobody would write a book ever again. Parliament didn't listen. They actually realised that public access to knowledge has a far bigger value than a distribution monopoly.'

With the establishment of radio regulations in the early twentieth century, a 'pirate' became someone who broadcast themselves without a licence. Pirate stations located their studios in boats: being in international waters, they were no longer subject to UK broadcasting law. The word soon evolved to encompass other media, from cassette-taped albums to ripped-off video games to, more recently, downloads of just about anything. This latter meaning was cemented in 2003 by the launch of infamous movie- and music-sharing site The Pirate Bay.

But Elston, the PPUK leader, emphasises that pirate politics are about more than entertainment, a key example being his party's wish to abolish drug patents. 'The NHS have to pay out for an extortionately high patent for a cancer or Alzheimer's drug,' he says, 'so we find if there was this sort of reform then the NHS wouldn't be forking out massive amounts on drug payments. They could put that money into better things.' (Critics note that this money can fund research.) Falkvinge proudly recalls that pirates have successfully fought copyright laws so as to enable books to be converted into formats that are accessible for the blind.

If there is a grand vision to pirate politics, it is to update democracy for the digital era.

In the 1970s, a British pirate radio DJ calling himself 'Prince Roy' set up a standalone micronation, Sealand, on a former military platform in the North Sea.

FLAGORAMA

The great sadness of the flag enthusiast, or vexillologist, is that when it comes to eighteenth-century, mast-based message design, most know the Jolly Roger and that's about it. Those banal crossed bones. That clichéd white skull. Has anything ever been more dreary? How much more elegance and subtlety in the flags of those who followed the rules, as per the beautiful panoply on display here.

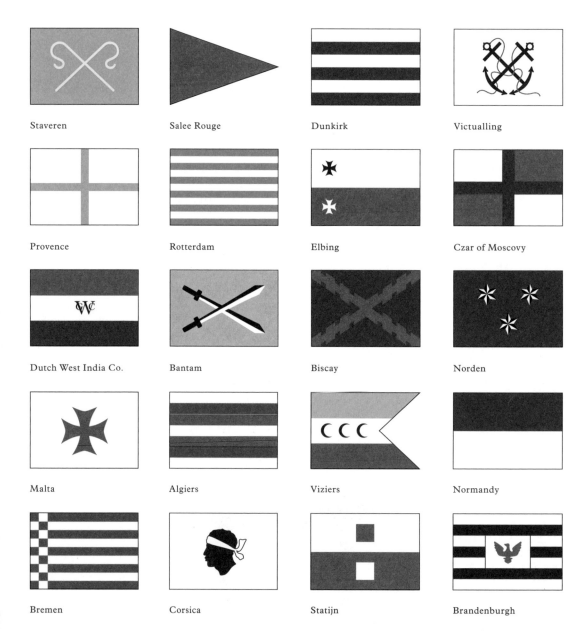

Staveren

Salee Rouge

Dunkirk

Victualling

Provence

Rotterdam

Elbing

Czar of Moscovy

Dutch West India Co.

Bantam

Biscay

Norden

Malta

Algiers

Viziers

Normandy

Bremen

Corsica

Statijn

Brandenburgh

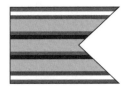

Sangrian

Algiers at War

Ostend

Burgundy

Ter Veer Jack

Sicily

Russia Galley

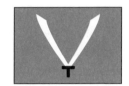

Salee

Scotch

Persia

Brabant

Konningsberg

Leghorne

Courland

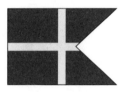

Swedes Common

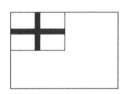

Picardy

Constantinople

Calais

Sardinia

Also Russia Galley

Heiligeland

Moores

Zeland

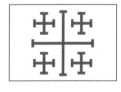

Jerusalem

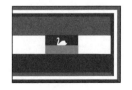

Waterland

Flag of Defiance

Grand Turk

Turks Galley

YO-HO-HO
This Grenadian rum is
still made according to
eighteenth-century meth-
ods rendering it, as they
put it, 'slightly overproof'.

The Icelandic Pirate Party's policies include making Iceland a safe haven for whistleblowers such as Edward Snowden, eliminating data retention and reforming mental illness services. 'Just basically human rights, with the angle of human rights being the same in the digital space,' explains founder Birgitta Jónsdóttir.

Thrice in our conversation, Falkvinge phrases one of the movement's key anxieties as follows: 'The big problem here is that our kids are not inheriting the civil liberties of our parents.' A central concern is privacy. In the UK, for example, the recent implementation of the Investigatory Powers Act means that dozens of governmental bodies, from the Food Standards Agency to the Metropolitan Police, can view a record of which websites you've visited in the last year. 'Our parents could buy a newspaper anonymously for cash on a newsstand on the corner, read whatever newspaper they liked, without the government knowing what articles they were reading, for how long, and in what order, and what they did next. Our kids no longer have that right.' Of course some might argue that those who want to maintain their privacy could still buy printed newspapers instead of reading them online, but the core point is that it's unfair that as technology progresses, our rights regress.

Falkvinge is a convincing speaker. After the first MEP was elected under his leadership in 2009, he stepped down and focused on being a spokesperson for the movement. 'I don't like paperwork,' he says. 'I have no interest in sitting on wooden benches and discussing social security. I'm entirely uninterested in power. Power is a means, not a goal.'

Many pirate parties feel the same. The pirate philosophy doesn't just inspire their policies but an entire methodology. They are proponents of direct democracy, which in practice means that they crowdsource their manifestos online and allow everyone to have their say. They staunchly believe in free speech and want to challenge the status quo of what they see as corrupt and ineffectual politics. Although, given their relative youth as a political movement, they have achieved immense electoral success, many pirates simply aim to get their issues noticed by parliament, rather than actually form a government themselves.

One party, however, has come very close to winning power. After existing for just four years, the Icelandic Píratar came third in the country's 2016 elections. 'We're sort of still processing this a little bit,' laughs Jónsdóttir, who remains its 'leader'.

Leader is in inverted commas here because Jónsdóttir, like many political pirates, doesn't believe in traditional governmental hierarchies. She refers to herself as a 'poetician' (Elston calls himself a 'parentician').

'I have never been interested in being a prime minister,' she says. 'If I could have been a prime minister I would have liked to reject it and say that I wanted to be the speaker of the house... I see the Pirate Party as a movement to get the general public to understand and recognise that nobody, not even a person that would have the title prime minster, is going to save them.'

And Jónsdóttir firmly believes that the world needs saving. The Píratar has succeeded where other pirate parties failed thanks to a distrust of traditional politics. This began after the 2008 financial crisis, and was exacerbated when their prime minister resigned last year after it was revealed in the Panama Papers that he sheltered money offshore.

She sees the pirate movement as an alternative to the nationalistic forms of populism that are currently upending the political status quo across the world. 'A lot of people have said that because there was a pirate party, that helped empower these people instead of bringing them to us, based on fear and patriotism and isolationism.

'The situation we have currently in our world is that people feel powerless. They feel afraid for the future. The tendency is that democracy suffers and people look for strong, dominant leaders — usually male chauvinists or people that are authoritarian. Now we offer something else, which is empowerment through the collective.'

If this sounds a little utopian, that's because it is — and it doesn't always work in practice. In its early years, the German Piratenpartei achieved rapid success, winning fifteen seats in the Berlin parliament during the 2011 state elections and gaining 35,000 members by the end of 2012. Yet by the time the next Berlin state elections rolled around in 2016, the party's membership had halved and it failed to win a single seat. Falkvinge claims the party was a victim of its own success, as its rapid expansion meant it couldn't keep its promise to give every member a vote on each issue. Yet the party has also been plagued by scandals, including a spokesman leaving in 2010 after being convicted for possessing child pornography, and a murder-suicide in 2016 committed by a former assembly member.

Falkvinge himself is no stranger to controversy. In 2010 he argued that child pornography should be decriminalised, and having initially backed away from his position after the resulting backlash, he now stands by it — arguing that these laws allow governments to justify surveillance while doing little to tackle paedophilia itself.

'They can pull this card and always get public opinion on their side,' he argues — noting that recently the FBI let a child pornographer go free as they did not want to explain to the court the surveillance methods they used to catch him.

'If child abuse imagery is being used to justify these surveillance methods, then the FBI choose to release an actual child pornographer because they don't want to disclose the methods used — then what is the real reason the surveillance is being used here?'

Despite such controversies, it is undeniable that pirate parties have seen immense success. After the October elections, the Píratir was invited to form a government, though ultimately was unable to find common ground with the necessary coalition partners. Falkvinge,

however, worries that things aren't changing fast enough.

'We're seeing the roll-out of surveillance states and my worry is that, yes, we're growing, but are we growing fast enough?' he says, noting that the UK's new Digital Economy Bill hopes to punish online pirates with ten years in prison ('That's more than rape!').

'It is quite possible that when enough people wake up to what is going on, it will be largely too late.'

Says Elston: 'It's not even a case where we're fighting for more rights now. We're actually fighting just to retain what we've got.'

Jónsdóttir is adamant that change is needed more than ever, but she respects that not everyone will see the Pirate Party as the solution. 'We live in very dangerous times,' she says. 'We have to wake up and we have to understand that democracy is work, so if you don't like what you see, go and do something.'

Whether you view piracy as equivalent to stealing a car, or are concerned by the current direction of politics, Jónsdóttir urges action.

'If we want to create our dream society, it is really up to us. Nobody is going to come save us except ourselves.'

AMELIA TAIT is the tech and digital culture writer at the *New Statesman*, where she writes about cyberpsychology, social media and memes. Her ideal treasure chest would include Bernard's Watch — a pocket watch that can stop time — and also loads of bags of Revels with the raisin ones taken out.

Hello! Everyone loves a talking, squawking parrot, right? Actually, discovers YELENA MOSKOVICH, these brilliant featherbrains have a long history not only of charming but of betraying their loyal owners. Pretty strange!

MY PARROT BETRAYED ME

Before the parrot took its place on a pirate's shoulder, or babbled in cartoons, the *Kama Sutra* listed teaching this bird to speak among its sixty-four arts of pleasurable living.

Possessing one of the highest intellects among all birds, with a brain-to-body size ratio comparable to that of higher primates, and exhibiting the social appetite of a three-year-old child, this chattering avian creature has been kept as a house pet for thousands of years, firstly by the upper classes in Asia and Africa, and then by the

Mosaic from the Vatican's dedicated parrot room.

European aristocracy, after Alexander the Great's army returned in 327 BC with a variety of ring-necked parrot known to this day as the 'Alexandrine parakeet'.

Marie Antoinette cherished her African grey, Queen Victoria's Coco sang 'God Save the Queen', and Pope Martin V appointed a Keeper of Parrots to look after his dearests, creating a dedicated parrot room — Camera di Pappagallo — at the Vatican for future parrot-doting popes. Steven Spielberg's darling is named Blanche, and fourteen US presidents have kept a talking bird of one species or another at the White House.

Amazingly, the parrot imitates speech without vocal chords, lips, teeth or palate (try saying 'b', 'm', 'p' or 'w' without using your lips), by squeezing its syrinx, located between the trachea and lungs, as air goes through; yet this has often been overshadowed by its ancient reputation for seeing — and repeating — what it should not. The Bible warns us of this time-worn tattletale who 'may carry your words [and] report what you say' (Ecclesiastes 10:20), and an old Basque legend paints the parrot as a perceptive bird, able to detect lies in children.

Today the parrot remains a beloved pet, but the privileged eye it casts over our human dramas, and its ability to replay the voices within them, has never diminished.

In 2006 in Leeds, Ziggy, an eight-year-old parrot belonging to a man named Chris, started making kissing sounds whenever the name Gary was spoken on TV, squawking out 'Hiya Gary' in imitation of his girlfriend Suzy's voice when her mobile phone rang and, finally, proclaiming à la Suzy, 'I love you, Gary!' Gary, Chris realised, was Suzy's ex-colleague — and current lover.

In 2016 in Kuwait, where infidelity is punishable by prison or hard labour, a wife brought in her bright-green rose-ringed parrot to the police, where he repeatedly mimicked her husband and their maid's voices in what *Al-Shahed* newspaper reported as a 'flirtatious exchange'.

A parrot proved to be a valuable crime witness in Sand Lake, Michigan, in 2015. Martin Duram and his wife, Glenna, were found shot — the former dead, the latter unconscious but alive. The sole witness

4. EYE
—
Thrasyllus of Mendes, chief astrologer to the Roman Emperor Tiberius, claimed that when the moon is the colour of a parrot's eye, one should expect immediate rain.

was Martin's parrot, Bud. The parents of the deceased overheard Bud yelling out an argument between Martin and Glenna (in their respective voices), finishing in Martin's voice, 'Don't f—ing shoot!' When Glenna awoke from her injury, she attested that she did not remember anything. After nearly a year of stalled investigations, Bud's testimony helped lead to Glenna's arrest.

Similarly, when Neelam Sharma and her dog were murdered in 2014 in Agra, India, the police were stumped. But then her husband noticed that their pet parrot, Hercule, would start screeching in panic at the mention of the name Ashutosh. When his nephew, Ashutosh, came to visit, things fell into place. During interrogation, Ashutosh confessed to killing his aunt when she had come across him trying to steal money and valuables from her home, and to stabbing the dog as it wouldn't stop barking. He'd overlooked Hercule, watching silently in his cage.

Last year, Evie, another devoted parrot, who had gone missing for over three weeks, hailed a cab to get back to her owner, Peter Jackson, in Tamworth, Staffordshire, who had acquired the bird for company after his wife passed away.

And when Guillermo Reyes, aged forty-nine, was pulled over at a routine checkpoint in Mexico City, his pet parrot, perched on the back seat, yelled out, 'He's drunk, he's drunk!' Reyes indeed failed the sobriety test. The officer arrested the man, who confessed to intoxication, but pleaded not to be separated from the bird. Eventually, police let the parrot accompany Reyes to jail.

YELENA MOSKOVICH is a Ukrainian-born American author and playwright living in Paris. Her debut novel is *The Natashas* (Serpent's Tail, 2016), and her plays have been produced in the US, Vancouver, Paris, and Stockholm. She's never dreamt of parrots, but has worked in an office with one, named Romeo.

FILM

So vivid are the word-images conjured up in *Treasure Island* that it can virtually lay claim itself to being the first ever pirate movie. As the *Pirates of the Caribbean* gear up for yet another outing, noted Stevenson expert NICHOLAS RANKIN looks at the myriad ways in which this adventure formula is forever being played out in movie theatres — and probably always will be. People really do love a pirate movie.

LONG JOHN SILVER SCREEN

Robert Louis Stevenson thought the process of consuming text should be 'absorbing and voluptuous', filling the mind with 'the busiest, kaleidoscopic dance of images', the words running 'in our ears like the noise of breakers', and the story repeating itself 'in a thousand coloured pictures to the eye.' All of this a decade before cinema was invented.

Stevenson's first novel began with a picture. In the wet summer of 1881, the thirty-year-old writer was helping his 12-year-old stepson Lloyd Osbourne with an 'art-gallery' in their rented Scottish cottage. One drawing was of an island. Stevenson took it and started elaborating and naming its features. Then he took it away upstairs: 'As I pored upon my

FIND THE HAPPY READER HOARD

This map is real. The *Happy Reader* hoard is out there somewhere, and you can be the first to reach it. Find the stash in the pictured isle using the clues therein. Among a bijou cache of keepsakes and trinkets, the trove contains instructions to claim the true hoard, a complete (and valuable) set of back issues of *The Happy Reader*, plus every former Book of the Season.

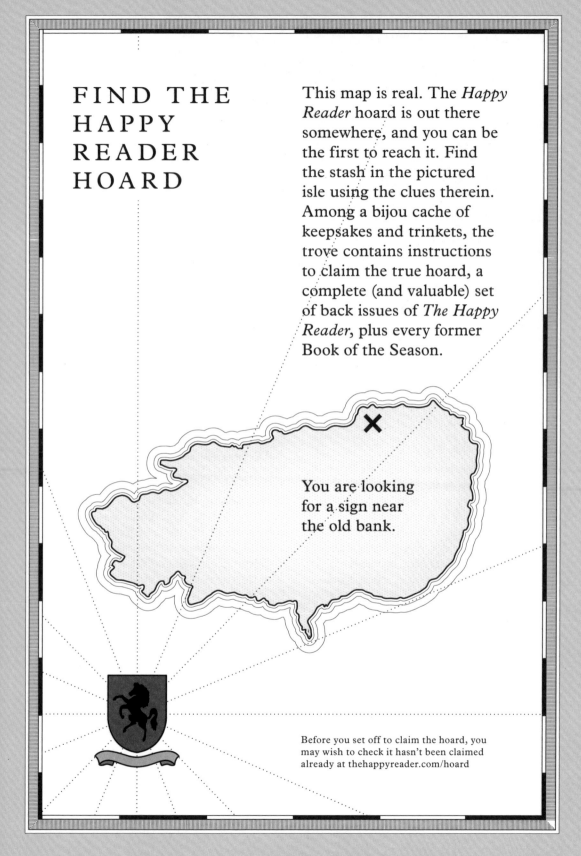

You are looking for a sign near the old bank.

Before you set off to claim the hoard, you may wish to check it hasn't been claimed already at thehappyreader.com/hoard

Kermit sails west as Captain Smollett in *Muppet Treasure Island*.

map of *Treasure Island*, the future characters of the book began to appear there visibly among imaginary woods; and their brown faces and bright weapons peeped out upon me from un-expected quarters, as they passed to and fro, fighting and hunting treasure, on these few square inches of a flat projection.'

Projection. In the century and a half since, grimy, grinning pirates have swarmed out of the silver screen. There have been over fifty film and TV adaptations of *Treasure Island*, including one with Orson Welles as Long John Silver, a role he relished. These films offer dramatically different takes. The 1937 Soviet version turned *Ostrov Sokrovisch* into a Marxist anti-imperialist adventure: the *Hispaniola* sails from Dublin seeking treasure to buy guns for Irish rebels of the 1790s. A Bulgarian sci-fi version made in 1982 was set in outer space.

Walt Disney stamped a particular mark on the genre. His 1950 adaptation of Stevenson's book was not Hollywood's first *Treasure Island* (Victor Fleming had directed Wallace Beery and Jackie Cooper in a very American black-and-white version in 1934), but it was the first live-action film that the inventor of Mickey Mouse made without any of his characteristic animations. Disney Studio's foreign revenues had been frozen in the Second World War meaning that by 1948 they had accumulated $850,000 to spend in the sterling area. Walt Disney went to Edinburgh to visit the museum in the house where Stevenson was born. An almost wholly British crew under US director Byron Haskin shot the film, in Technicolor, in Devon, Cornwall and the Bristol Channel, with interiors at Denham Studios. The great Freddie Young was the cinematographer.

For British viewers, the cast of the 1950 *Treasure Island* is full of familiar late-twenti-eth-century stalwarts including John Laurie (from Hitchcock's *The Thirty-Nine Steps* and later *Dad's Army*) as Blind Pew and Patrick Troughton (the second *Doctor Who*) as the wounded snarling pirate who tries to skewer Jim in the stockade. Among the actors cast in the buccaneer roles is Sam Kydd, at that time not long out of five years in a German PoW camp, and doomed ever after to portray 'other ranks' on screen.

Dominating it all, however, is the Dorset-born drunk and hell-raiser Robert Newton, playing Long John Silver. 'He was very tall and strong', wrote Stevenson of his duplicitous character, 'with a face as big as a ham — plain and pale but intelligent and smiling.' Newton, who had played Bill Sikes in David Lean's film of *Oliver Twist*, seems to have taken 'ham' as his cue, and his performance has duly stumped its way into popular culture. Newton's West Country accent ('Aaaar, Jim lad!') has made him the role-model for International Talk Like a Pirate Day (19 September every year), though you may also imitate Brian Blessed, Jack Palance or Eddie Izzard if you wish.

'As soon as Walt rode on a camera crane,' said one of his animators in 1950, 'we knew we were going to lose him.' Not entirely, but in the decade that followed Disney did make five times as many live action adventure films and nature documentaries as cartoons: *Robin Hood*, *Rob Roy*, *Captain Nemo*, *Zorro*, *Davy Crockett* and sundry westerns, and young Sean Connery the juve lead in the Irish fantasy *Darby O'Gill* and the *Little People*.

Restless Walt Disney wanted to create a cross between the cartoon and the live actor, and set his 'Imagineers' to work on realistic robots using what he termed 'audioanimatronics.' President Abraham Lincoln accordingly moved and talked again at the 1964–5 New York World's Fair. The last attraction that Disney devised before he died in December 1966 was a flume ride at Disneyland in California, called 'Pirates of the Caribbean', an experience that began with the skeletons of dead buccaneers and went on to feature three-dimensional life-size figures moving a bit, shooting pistols and cannons, 'fighting and hunting treasure' (and auctioning wenches) as the punters floated past.

There were two good *Treasure Island*s on the big screen in the 1990s. Charlton Heston made a convincingly villainous Silver in a vigorous (and faithful) version directed by his son Fraser Heston, in which a rousing score by The Chieftains augments cameos from Oliver Reed as Billy Bones and Christopher Lee as Blind Pew. 16-year-old Christian Bale was the right age to play Jim Hawkins, and went on to make the transition to adult actor far better than poor Bobby Driscoll, the 13-year-old child star of the 1950 Disney version, who died a destitute junkie aged 31.

Then there was *Muppet Treasure Island*. Co-produced by Disney, this affectionate parody version of Stevenson's book benefited from a deft script and songs like 'Professional Pirate' performed in the best panto style by Tim Curry as Long John Silver. The mixture of actors and Muppets — Billy Connolly is Black Dog but Kermit the Frog is Captain Smollett and Miss Piggy is 'Benjamina Gunn' — works well. The running jokes and knowing comments on the script keep jaded adults and Stevenson scholars amused: like *Treasure Island* itself, *Muppet Treasure Island* is not really for children.

That said, the 1990s were a troublesome time for the the the pirate film genre. Stephen Spielberg's *Hook* did not do as well as expected and the hugely expensive *Cutthroat Island* with Geena Davis and Matthew Modine bombed at the box-office, as did Disney's sci-fi animation *Treasure Planet* a few years later.

So it came as a surprise when the idea of turning that old 1967 Disneyland flume ride into a movie took off so spectacularly. Hans Zimmer, who wrote the music for *Muppet Treasure Island*, billowed sails again with a big romantic score, and the *Pirates of the Caribbean* franchise with Johnny Depp as Captain Jack Sparrow has, from 2002, proved an extraordinary treasure chest, with the first four films earning some $3.7 billion world-wide, and a fifth adding the latest entry to *Treasure Island*'s tottering cinematic legacy this summer. Why have the *Pirates of the Caribbean* films worked so well for the Disney empire? Action and romance in part, but mostly by mating comedy with horror in a new way. Robert Louis Stevenson's pirates were frightening and murderous, but also childishly superstitious, terrified of the dead. That has been seized on. And because digital technology can now make the supernatural realistic, these pirates, themselves resurrected from what seemed a moribund genre, can now move plausibly with the zombie undead on the flat projection of Jim Hawkins's 'accursed island'.

NICHOLAS RANKIN is a former BBC World Service journalist who has written five books for Faber & Faber. The first of these, *Dead Man's Chest: Travels after Robert Louis Stevenson* (1987), took him on a literary pilgrimage through Scotland, England, France, the United States, to Fiji, Australia and Western Samoa, where Stevenson is buried at the top of Mount Vaea on the island of Upolu.

OLD ROPE?
No, a single braid of
rope tobacco. Quite
unfashionable these days.
This and other objects
inspired by *Treasure
Island* photographed by
IVAN RUBERTO.

LETTERS

A spooky circle of literary luck, and a chance encounter with a certain map.

Dear Happy Reader,

Coincidence. I buy *THR8* for the cover Kristin Scott Thomas interview (I'm a big fan). Read the interviews (there are two) and Kristin loves Donna Tartt's *The Goldfinch* as I do (as I do all her books).

When Donna was on tour in London for *The Goldfinch* I attended an evening with her and asked if coincidence played a part in her writing as it always does in mine. She said it certainly did and in a conversation afterwards she spoke more on this and wrote me a treasured line in my copy: 'For Keith, who sees coincidences everywhere as I do'.

Kristin also says in *The Happy Reader* interviews that she buys her books at Shakespeare and Company, the revered bookshop in Paris (where she lives), which is where I bought the magazine while browsing the store — one of the best places on the planet. Coincidence.

It made me a happy reader.

Best wishes,
Keith Bradbrook
Kent, UK

Dear editor,

I'm only writing this letter on the off chance that I will win a free book. I've never won anything before. However, when we were children my sister did win a BBQ, but that's as far as chance gains have ever gotten in my family. I should also mention that I am not always a happy reader. Sometimes I'm sad or angry, quite often apoplectic; but mostly as a reader I find myself transfixed by the beauty and intricacy of the ideas of others, or transported to alternate worlds and ways of being. And when I'm lucky, the way in which I perceive and think about the world is transformed, sometimes by subtle means, sometimes through sheer malevolent force. Reading should be, and at its best is, transformational. So any enterprise which nurtures, mediates or supports our various paths through life, all astonishing in their own way, by offering us a chance to be so transformed, gets my vote; or in this case my $5.99; whether I get a free book or not.

Yours,
R. J. Mulholland
South of the Equator

Dear The Happy Reader,

I am excited to hear that you are starring Treasure Island in *THR9*. The day before *THR8* arrived, I had been to a great exhibition of maps at the National Library of Scotland. By coincidence I bought a postcard of a sketch map of *Treasure Island* by RLS himself. And separately I often look at the statue of Davy Balfour and Alan Breck from *Kidnapped*, on Corstorphine Road, Edinburgh. I wish it was in Herriot Row near his childhood home instead of on a piece of road that few people walk along.

Best regards,
Deirdre Forsyth
Edinburgh, Scotland

Send your thoughts on the issue and/or Books of the Season to letters@thehappyreader.com or The Happy Reader, Penguin Books, 80 Strand, London WC2R 0RL. If yours makes the issue, you'll not only see your name immortalised in black ink, you'll also receive a free copy of next Season's Book.

The Happy Reader is a book club like no other, one that gathers twice a year via the medium of a printed magazine. Join by subscribing — simply follow the instructions at thehappyreader.com.

A GREAT READ FOR WINTER

One way of thinking about any issue of *The Happy Reader* is that it's as if a book has sprung to life and taken up a position as a magazine editor. What reportage will it commission? What photography will it call in? Does it want a recipe page?

This coming winter our guest editor — the Book of the Season — is a work of dystopian fiction set in the twenty-sixth century AD, a book that was banned by a country that no longer exists. It's *We*, the best-known novel of dissident Russian author Yevgeny Zamyatin.

Zamyatin wrote *We* between 1920 and 1921, and although it was published in most of the world's languages shortly afterwards, it was the first book to be banned by the Soviet Union Censorship Board after the country was founded in 1923. It would not appear in the original Russian until 1988. Meanwhile it influenced writers such as George Orwell, Aldous Huxley and Ayn Rand. Ursula K. LeGuin described it as 'the best single work of science fiction yet written.' The story of a citizen (a mathematician named D-503) in a society where both privacy and individuality are relics of the past, *We* retains an eerie relevance. It's also just a really great read.

The next issue of *The Happy Reader* will be arriving on doorsteps and newsstands sometime between the changing of the clocks and the arrival of winter solstice. Readers wishing to remain aligned with the Book of the Season should track down Yevgeny Zamyatin's novel before then. Do ping us a line with any thoughts or impressions by emailing letters@thehappyreader.com.

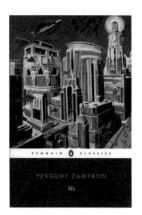

Jacket for *We*, originally published in English in 1924.